A Mother's Wish

A Mother's Wish

By KATHY-JO WARGIN

Illustrated by IRENA ROMAN

HarperCollinsPublishers

A Mother's Wish

Text copyright © 2006 by Kathy-jo Wargin

Illustrations copyright © 2006 by Irena Roman

Manufactured in China.

For information address HarperCollins Children's Books, a
division of HarperCollins Publishers, 1350 Avenue of the
Americas, New York, NY 10019.
www.harperchildrens.com

Library of Congress Cataloging-in-Publication Data

Wargin, Kathy-jo.   A mother's wish / by Kathy-jo Wargin ;
illustrated by Irena Roman.— 1st ed.   p.   cm.

Summary: A young girl and her mother both make secret wishes on
butterfly wings, and learn years later that the legend of the butterfly
is real and that both of their wishes have come true.

ISBN-10: 0-06-057170-5 — ISBN-10: 0-06-057171-3 (lib. bdg.)
ISBN-13: 978-0-06-057170-2 — ISBN-13: 978-0-06-057171-9 (lib. bdg.)

[1. Mothers and daughters—Fiction. 2. Wishes—Fiction.
3. Butterflies—Fiction.] I. Roman, Irena, ill. II. Title.

PZ7.W234Aam 2006   2004030200

[E]—dc22   CIP   AC

Typography by Carla Weise

1 2 3 4 5 6 7 8 9 10

❖

First Edition

To my beautiful mother,
Carol Nelson-Kelly,
who gave me wings to fly.
—K.J.W.

For Rosie and the Chief,
always in my heart.
—I.R.

Early one morning, Ella and her mother were picking flowers when a butterfly landed nearby.

"Do you know the legend of the butterfly?" asked Ella's mother. "If you whisper your greatest wish to a butterfly and send it on its way, the butterfly will carry your words high up into the sky. When your words reach the stars, your wish will come true."

Ella and her mother
brought the flowers into
the kitchen and put
them in a glass jar.
Ella was happy being
with her mother, and
she wanted that feeling
to last as long as
it could.

"Will you be my mother forever?" asked Ella.

"Yes, Ella," her mother replied.

"Will you be my mother even when I am big?" Ella asked again.

"Yes, I will still be your mother when you are big."

"Will you always be
my mother?"
"Yes," she said quietly,
"I will always be your
mother."

Ella thought about
what her mother had
said. She liked knowing
that her mother would
never go away.

Still thinking about
her mother's words,
Ella ran out of the
house the next morning
and back to the field
where they had walked
together the day before.
She spotted a butterfly
resting on a flower.

She gently cupped her hands around it and whispered,

"I make this wish on wings of love
And send into the sky above
That Mother holds me every day
And never, ever goes away."

She even wrote her wish
down and tucked it into a pink
box she kept on her dresser.

The days turned into months,
and the months turned into
years. As Ella grew older, she
never forgot about her butterfly
wish. In time, the small girl
who had wished on a butterfly
grew up beautiful and strong
like her mother.

"Ella, you are growing up so fast," said Ella's mother. "Soon it will be time to leave home."

"I know," said Ella thoughtfully, "but long ago I made a wish upon a butterfly."

Ella rummaged through her
dresser drawer and found the
pink box. She took out the note
that she had written long ago
and handed it to her mother.

I make this wish on wings of love
And send into the sky above
That Mother holds me every day
And never, ever goes away.

Ella's mother held her close in her arms. "Years ago," she said, "when you were a little girl, I too made a wish upon a butterfly."

Ella's mother handed
her daughter an old piece
of paper.

I wish to give you
wings to fly.
Wings to soar across the sky.
I wish to give you
wings to see
That you were made
for flying free.

"You see, Ella, a mother's wish is to see her daughter soar. Both of our wishes have come true, because no matter where you are, I will always be with you."

With that, Ella and her mother looked out the window and saw hundreds of butterflies fill the sky. All of them were beautiful and strong, and they all carried wishes on butterfly wings.